NORMAN BRIDWELL

Clifford®
VISITS THE HOSPITAL

SCHOLASTIC INC.

New York Toronto London Auckland Sydney
Mexico City New Delhi Hong Kong

To Carly, Perry, Griffin,
and Tess Elizabeth

The author thanks Manny Campana
for his contribution to this book.

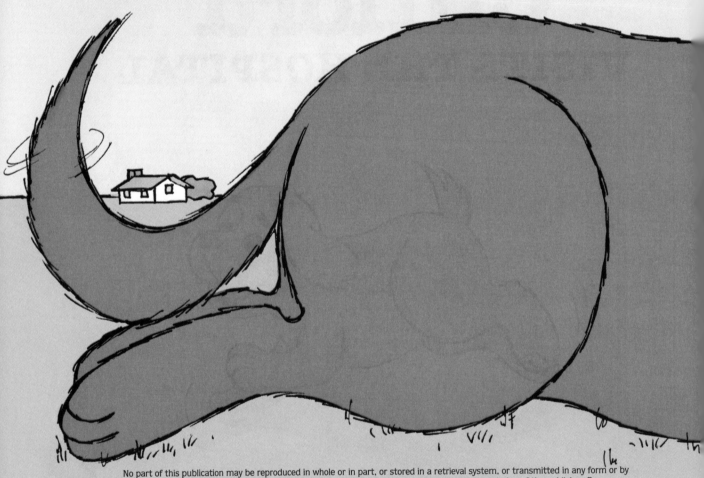

ISBN 0-439-14096-X
Copyright © 2000 by Norman Bridwell.
All rights reserved. Published by Scholastic Inc.
SCHOLASTIC, CARTWHEEL BOOKS and associated logos are trademarks and/or registered trademarks of Scholastic Inc.
CLIFFORD, CLIFFORD THE BIG RED DOG, CLIFFORD THE SMALL RED PUPPY,
and associated logos are trademarks and/or registered trademarks of Norman Bridwell.

10 9 8 7 6 5   5 6 7 8 9/0
Printed in the U.S.A.
First printing, August 2000

I'm Emily Elizabeth, and this is my dog, Clifford.
When he was a puppy, Clifford went to the hospital.

Clifford wasn't sick. He went accidentally. My grandma
was in the hospital, and Mom made some cookies for her.

Clifford loves cookies. When we weren't looking,
he jumped into the basket.

At the hospital, Grandma thanked us for the treat.
Then she said she'd like something to read while she
munched a cookie.

So Mom and I went down to the gift shop to get
her a magazine.

What a surprise! Grandma loved having Clifford come to visit her, but dogs are not allowed in the hospital.

Suddenly, Grandma heard footsteps. The nurse was coming! What would the nurse do when she saw Clifford?

Luckily, the nurse didn't see him. He was too small.

The nurse had come to check Grandma's
pulse and take her temperature.

To Clifford, the thermometer looked like a stick of peppermint candy.

Ugh! That was <u>not</u> candy. It tasted like medicine!

Grandma didn't have a chance to tell the nurse that
a dog had just licked the thermometer. Yuck!

The nurse had to give Grandma a shot. That's when Clifford decided to leave. He hates needles.

Clifford zigzagged through people's feet
in the busy hallway.

He sped around a corner and dashed
through an open door.

The children were amazed to see a small red puppy
in the hospital.

The children had lots of fun playing with Clifford.
Clifford was having fun, too.
And then...

some girls started to dress him up like a doll.

Clifford couldn't wait to get out of there.

Clifford was in such a hurry, he didn't look where he was going.

What a mess!

One of the children came to the rescue.

He found a nice, safe place for Clifford.

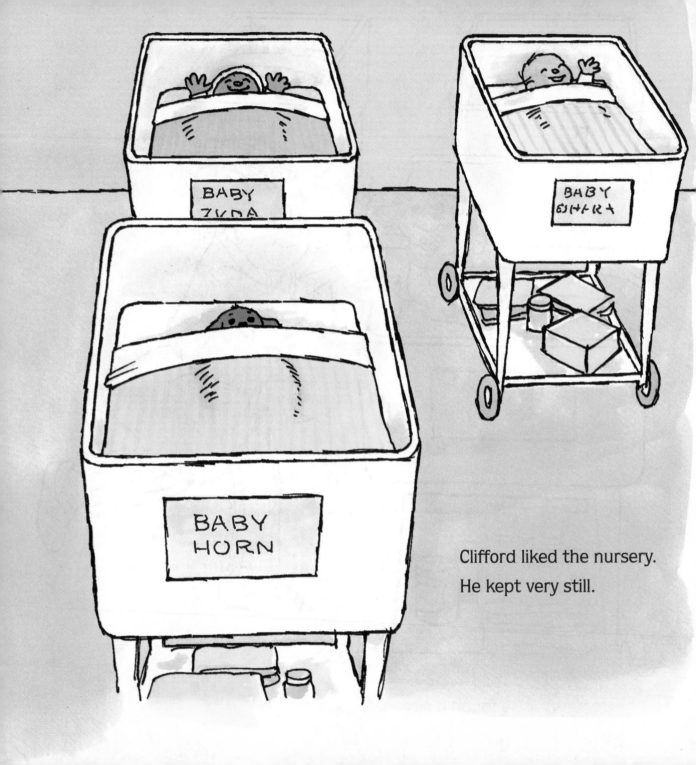

Clifford liked the nursery.
He kept very still.

A proud new father came to the window and asked
to see his beautiful baby. Uh-oh!

NURSERY

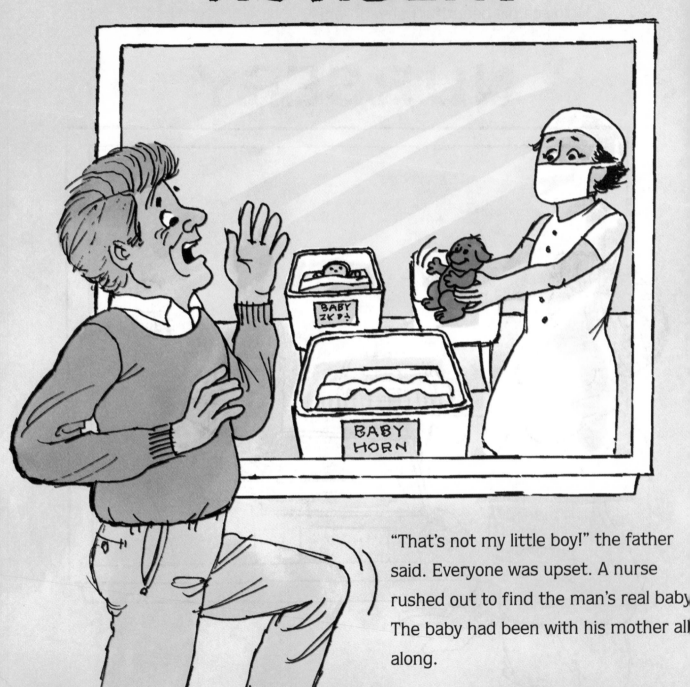

"That's not my little boy!" the father said. Everyone was upset. A nurse rushed out to find the man's real baby. The baby had been with his mother all along.

Just then, Mom and I came back from the gift shop.
We told the nurse and doctor that we would take
Clifford home right after we said good-bye to Grandma.

Grandma was sorry that Clifford couldn't stay.

But she was happy with the new dog we found for her
in the gift shop. This one wouldn't run away.

Now Clifford goes to the hospital from time to time
to visit his friends and make them feel better.
Good old Clifford.